ISBN: 978-1-7350319-5-8 Library of Congress Catalog Number: 2022930866 Printed in China First Printing: 2022 25 24 23 22   5 4 3 2 1 Book design and typesetting by Tejas Soni. Bree Serif Sofia Pro Cubano Published in the United States of America by Modern Marigold Books, LLC, Waxhaw, NC, in 2022. For ordering information, visit www.ModernMarigoldBooks.com

FSC
www.fsc.org
MIX
Paper from responsible sources
FSC® C144853

To all the wonderful women in my life who have made me feel confident in my own skin. Especially my amazing mother and big sister. You both have shown me what it means to be beautiful inside and out.
— F.F.

"For Baji Cheepees and a very special potato."
— A.S.

BASKING
IN MY
BROWN

WRITTEN BY
FATIMA FAISAL

ILLUSTRATED BY
ANAIN SHAIKH

MODERN MARIGOLD BOOKS

SWEET SUMMERTIME.

I love how the warm breeze brings fond memories of days spent flying kites on empty rooftops while visiting Dada in Pakistan.

I love the outdoor dinner parties Ammi puts together, everyone's kurtas sparkling brilliantly under the twinkling stars.

I love swimming in deep, cool water and building castles that are my own.

I love climbing trees—strong and grand—grown, just like me.

But most of all,
I LOVE BASKING IN THE SUN.

Today, Zoya and I play
under a bright blue sky,

the sun coating us in gold.

We close our eyes and
feel the warmth sink in.

When the sun is high in the sky, Zoya stands up. "I should go in," she sighs.

"So soon?" I ask.

"My mom says I shouldn't stay out in the sun too long.

That it'll make my skin get too dark," Zoya replies, shaking off the blades of grass that cling to her legs.

"Will you go in, too?"

"I am going to stay out all day," I proudly declare.

"I love watching my skin turn all different shades of brown. My mom says the sun makes my skin a magical brown."

"A magical brown?" Zoya asks.

I hold out my hand.

The sun beams down on my skin, basking in my brown.

"See how it shimmers?"

"My skin is **BROWN,**
like the heavy clay pot from my Nani's
stories, filled to the top with cool water.

Water she carried in the hot sun for miles
and miles, to bring back to her family."

"BROWN, like the shawl that kept Ammi warm as she and Abbu journeyed above the clouds, from their homeland to a land we now call our home."

"BROWN, like the henna my sister draws on her hands.

Each pattern, special in its own way.
Soft flowers, hugging strong vines."

"**BROWN,** like the perfectly round gulab jamuns Khala makes, dancing in sticky syrup, golden flakes floating on top.

My favorite dessert, sweet and bold with flavor."

"BROWN, like the packed soil of the cricket pitch, the one where Abbu used to play.

Soil, so sturdy and sound."

"**BROWN,** like the bangles I wear.
They jingle and jangle, singing

'I AM PROUD TO BE ME!'"

My brown skin has its own story:

it is **STRONG**

it is **AMBITIOUS**

it is **BOLD**

it is **SOFT**

it is **SWEET**

it is **FEARLESS**

It is a beautiful brown.

It is my very own beautiful brown.

"Wow!" Zoya says in awe. She thinks a moment longer before lying back down in the grass.

"I'm staying," she smiles. "I like the idea of this magic."

We sprawl our arms and legs out as wide as we can, ready to add to our story and proudly bask in our brown.

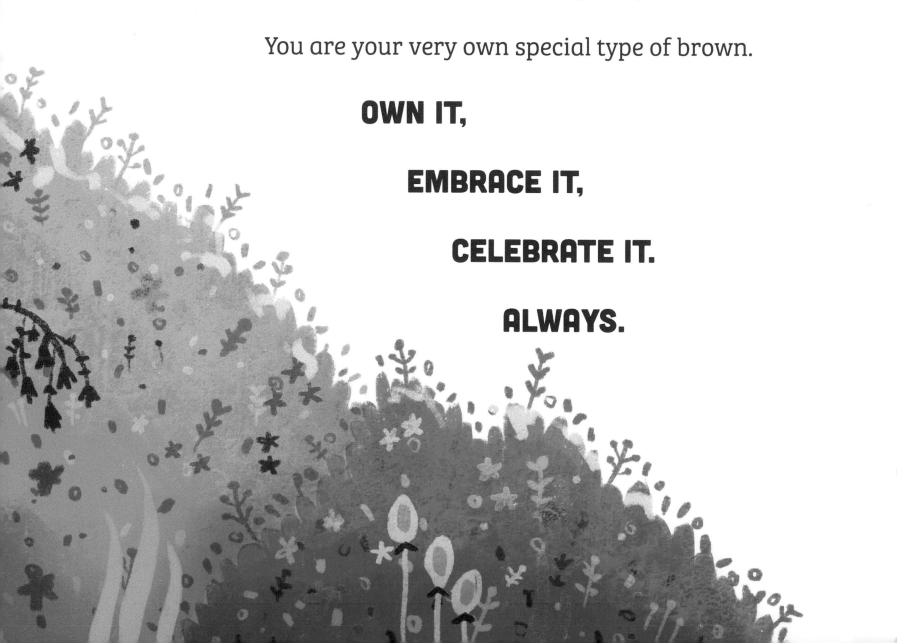

Dear beautiful brown girls,

Never forget who you are and where you came from. It is what makes you special.

You are your very own special type of brown.

OWN IT,

EMBRACE IT,

CELEBRATE IT.

ALWAYS.